A Moose's Morning

By Pamela Love
Illustrated by Lesia Sochor

Down East Books

Library of Congress Cataloging-in-Publication Data
Love, Pamela.
  A moose's morning / by Pamela Love ; illustrated by Lesia Sochor.
    p. cm.
  ISBN-13: 978-0-89272-733-9 (trade hardcover : alk. paper)
  ISBN-10: 0-89272-733-0
  1. Moose—Infancy—Juvenile literature. 2. Moose—Juvenile literature.
I. Sochor, Lesia, 1952- ill. II. Title.
  QL737.U55L685 2007
  599.65'7139—dc22
                          2006021072

Book Design by Lindy Gifford
Printed in China

5   4   3   2   1

Down East Books
A division of Down East Enterprise, Inc.,
publisher of *Down East*, the Magazine of Maine

Distributed to the trade by National Book Network

Book orders: 1-800-685-7962   www.downeastbooks.com

To Elaine and Arlo Barnard, my aunt and uncle.

— P.L.

For all members of the animal kingdom.

— J.S.

It was just after a summer sunrise. Half-hidden by reeds, a moose calf watched his mother. She stood in a lake, eating underwater plants. Often the calf could see only her back.

Whenever the cow moose did lift her head, her nostrils opened wide. Each breath brought her two things: air and information. From their scents, she knew which animals were close by.

For now, there was nothing dangerous. She returned to her browsing.

The calf also kept alert. His big brown eyes and bigger brown ears were always searching for danger.

Spotting another moose across the lake, the calf stared. He'd never seen an adult bull before. The stranger's antlers, still covered in protective velvet, were wider than the calf was long.

The bull moose had pulled off every twig and leaf he could reach from the lower part of a young white birch tree. But he was still hungry. He walked forward, shoving the trunk of the sapling with his chest.

Crick, crack, cree-eak… Finally the birch went over with a soft thump. The bull moose began eating the remaining leaves, which were now within his reach.

With her next breath, the calf's mother learned about the other moose. Not trusting the stranger, she left the lake. Water drizzled out of her drooping ears.

The hungry calf nursed while his mother kept watch. After her calf had finished feeding, the mother moose led him away until they reached a willow. Still hungry, she began munching.

It had rained the night before. Puddles lay around the tree. The calf smacked one with a hoof. Splashing was fun!

Trotting around the willow, he stamped in each puddle.

Without realizing it, he was moving away from his mother. At the same time, without his thinking about it, his ears twisted and turned, listening for trouble.

Snap! A twig broke, followed by an excited Yip! Bawling, the calf fled, three coyotes at his heels.

Bellowing, the mother moose charged, her hooves lashing out. The coyotes were dangerous, but she could be, too.

Their chance at an easy meal gone, the coyotes whirled on their heels and disappeared into the forest.

Meanwhile, the moose calf kept on running. Just ahead of him was a low branch, where a fisher was snapping at a porcupine's face. Although he tried to dodge it, the calf still bumped the branch. The fisher swung around to hiss at him.

That was a mistake. By the time the fisher turned back to his prey, the porcupine had hidden her face against a hollow in the tree. Her quill-filled tail lashed back and forth. Disappointed, the fisher dropped to the ground and headed away.

Soon the cow moose had caught up with her calf. His heart was still pounding from his run, but his mother began calmly stripping leaves off a nearby branch. Gradually, the calf relaxed. Surely nothing would dare hurt him while he was so close to her. He began nibbling, using his sensitive nose to find the most tender leaves.

Whirr! Something feathery burst upward from the ground, just ahead of him. With a squeaky cry, the calf stumbled back against his mother.

Instantly, she trotted off, the young moose close beside her. She would have known the ruffed grouse wasn't dangerous, but in the wild, running is often safer than investigating.

The calf had to go around bushes that his mother went right through, but he didn't fall behind.

The sun was high overhead when the two moose stopped at another lake. The cow sniffed, and listened hard. All was peaceful. She led her calf into the water. This time, instead of dunking for food, she headed for a small island.

Tired from the morning's excitement, the calf rested his chin on his mother's back as they swam.

He stumbled slightly when he climbed onto the island. Just as he reached a patch of soft, green moss, his legs folded up. Moments later, his mother touched his face gently with her nose. The calf didn't notice. He had fallen sound asleep.

Moose Facts

They can beat you in a swimming race. They can beat you in a foot race. And that's when they're only one week old. What are they? Moose calves!

Besides its speed, a moose calf depends on his mother for protection. Few animals are more dangerous than a mother moose (called a cow) that is protecting her calf. People should always keep their distance from moose, but especially from one who has one or more calves. Cow moose can outsprint Olympic track stars.

A moose calf stays with its mother until it's about twelve months old. By that point, the mother has taught her youngster enough that it can live on its own. A male calf will start growing his antlers at this time.

Only male moose grow antlers, but they don't keep them all year. The antlers fall off in the late autumn, sometimes one at a time. (A one-antlered moose looks really strange!) They grow back in the spring, a little larger each year until the moose has reached its full size. Antlers can be wider than most adult humans are tall—up to six feet.